CHRISTMAS GIVE
A Holiday Novella

By Meda White

This is a work of fiction. Names, characters, places and occurrences are a product of the author's imagination. Any resemblance to actual persons, living or dead, places or occurrences, is purely coincidental.

CHAPTER ONE

Eva Walker stuck her head in the back door of her cousin's house and felt the weight of a dozen eyes. "Santa's spy checking to see who's being naughty."

"Cuz." Brad scooped her into a bone crushing hug. "Why are you sneaking in the back and why are you so late? I expected you hours ago."

"My cell phone died, and I thought I'd slip in when I realized you're having a party. Did I get the dates wrong? I thought the party was tomorrow."

"The real party is tomorrow. Tonight is a pre-party." A blonde woman extended her free hand. "I'm Brad's girlfriend, Portia."

Eva tried not to flinch away from the offered hand because the inch-long, jewel encrusted fingernails looked like weapons. "Is that your Porsche out front?"

"I wish." She put her arm around Brad. "What are you wearing?"

Eva glanced down at her green fleece track suit and noticed the paw prints on her chest. It was comfortable attire for a nine-hour drive, but not appropriate for an unexpected pre-Christmas-party party. "Just the love and fur of a rough coat collie." She brushed herself off.

"You met Bella." Brad's smile lit up his face. "Isn't she gorgeous? She's normally inside, but Portia didn't want her dress to get covered with dog hair."

Eva's mouth twitched with irony over the girl's wardrobe choice. "What poor creature are you wearing?"

Portia must've been a real blonde like the ones they make the jokes about because she took a long moment before she stroked her fur shrug. "Oh, this is a mink."

Eva forced a straight face. "You kill it yourself?"

"Huh?"

Brad's laughter rang out. "She's just teasing you, babe. I told you she was a cut-up."

A honking brute of a man with shaggy dark hair and a dazzling smile stepped beside Eva and took her suitcase. "Nice to finally meet you."

Her smile widened when she recognized his deep voice. "Adam." She gave him a tentative hug.

"He goes by Mack, cuz."

They'd talked on the phone a few times when Eva called to make arrangements to stay with Brad for Christmas. Adam was a college buddy of Brad's who was considering relocating to Atlanta for work, so Brad had invited him to stay for Christmas.

No one had told her he was the size of Rhode Island or that he was hotter than hell's waiting room. She'd also never heard the name Mack before, except for Brad's college teammate, Mack Riggs, who went on to have a successful career in the NFL.

This couldn't be the same guy, but he was big enough to be. She rubbed her eyes in an attempt to clear her muddled brain.

"Come on. I'll show you to your room and you can freshen up." Adam extended a hand toward the hallway.

She walked and tried not to be self-conscious that he followed. She probably had doggy paws on her backside, too.

"You're on the left. I'm right across the hall, and we're sharing the bathroom. I hope you don't mind." He followed her into the bedroom and put her luggage on the bed. "Brad was going to give you his room until Portia pitched a fit."

"Goodness, that boy needs me to screen his

dates."

"I think he's hoping you'll move back to the area and help him find the right woman."

"So he knows she's wrong for him and he's with her anyway?"

Adam/Mack bit his lower lip. She recognized it as a gesture she did when she was trying to hold back a painfully honest response.

"I get it. Free milk."

He threw his head back and laughed. Goose bumps rose on her skin as the deep rumble ran through her.

"I'm sorry. That was openly inappropriate. I'll try to rein it in."

"Don't hold back on my account. Can I get you anything? Water? Wine?"

Her shoulders fell forward, and she grabbed his arm. "Oh, thank you. I'd love some water. I'm dehydrated because I drink as little as possible on road trips…fewer pit stops."

"I'll be right back." He shook his head as he walked away.

Eva rifled through her bag for her toiletry kit and clothes before she dashed into the bathroom. Her toothbrush was hanging out of her mouth while she struggled into the world's smallest spandex body slip. It was guaranteed to reduce your body by two dress sizes.

A mixture of foamy toothpaste and saliva fell out of her mouth onto her thigh. At least that body part would smell minty fresh if anyone fell asleep with their head in her lap.

A memory of her husband gripped her with such force, she had to sit down before she fell.

***

Adam "Mack" Riggs stood outside the closed bathroom door, holding a bottle of water. He should just leave it in her room and give her some space, but he'd told a partial untruth involving her and thought it'd be wise to fill her in.

He knocked on the door. "Room service."

"Just a sec."

There was all manner of strange noises coming from the bathroom: something being dropped, water running, body parts hitting the wall followed by swearing, but instead of curse words, they were words one heard at the holidays—tangled tinsel, stuffed stockings, and charred chestnuts.

He smiled.

He'd liked Eva from their first conversation. It'd been nice talking to someone who didn't have expectations or preconceived ideas about him, which was why he'd given her his real name. He wasn't the most famous defensive back to ever play the game, but people who followed the NFL normally recognized his name, especially after the unwelcome notoriety following him getting axed and his wife's affair with another team's quarterback, which led to the divorce he hadn't planned on. Even after her betrayal, he still loved her. The press had thought it was great celebrity gossip. He thought his life was falling apart.

He'd been dreading his first Christmas as a single man in more than twelve years. That was until he'd answered Brad's phone one day and discovered a sweet Southern accent attached to a sassy woman who made him laugh. He'd missed Renee a little less since that day.

The door opened and eyes the color of an evergreen looked out at him. The pictures he'd seen of her had revealed a big smile and a twinkle in her eyes, but seeing her in three dimensions was even better. What the photos had failed to show was that she wasn't much taller than one of Santa's elves. However, the curve-hugging dress she wore gave him caveman thoughts of tossing her over his shoulder and carrying her to the North Pole. If Santa were a caveman... There was the beard...

Changing the direction of his thoughts, he twisted the lid to break the seal before handing the water bottle to her.

"You're a lifesaver." She drank half the liquid before she paused to catch her breath.

He watched her chest heave under the gray sweater dress before he forced his gaze back to her face. "You've got a little..." He reached and wiped toothpaste from the corner of her mouth.

"Hey, I wasn't done with that." She grabbed his hand and stopped shy of licking the tip of his finger. "Oh goodness, I don't know where your finger's been."

He laughed. "No place terribly disgusting, I hope."

"Would you tell me if you'd just been picking your nose?"

"Probably not."

It was her turn to laugh, and she clutched her stomach. "I can't breathe."

When she turned toward the sink, he understood why. The back of her dress was hung up on her Spanx, or whatever Lycra-laced undergarment the women were wearing these days.

"Let me just help you out here." He pulled the hem of her dress down until her slip was hidden from view.

"Can I embarrass myself any more?" She kept her back to him and placed makeup on the counter. It was only five or six items, whereas Renee had about fifty, which had covered the entire bathroom counter.

"Nothing to be ashamed over. Wardrobe malfunctions happen."

"I guess I should be grateful I wasn't singing at a halftime show, flashing the world my back side. Sorry about that."

"No worries, it was covered." *Sadly*. He hesitated a second. "Listen, you're not upset with me, are you? For not telling you who I really am, or was? I'm not really Mack anymore."

"So, you *are* the best cornerback to ever play the game?" She tilted her head to the side, making eye contact in the mirror.

His mouth hung open, and he almost missed her wink. Her words did something to him, touched a deep place he'd forgotten. It wasn't just what she said, but how—with a conviction no one could doubt.

"Is Mack even your real name?"

He shook his head. "No. It started in high school. They said I hit like a Mack truck and with a last name like Riggs, it stuck."

"I think I can understand where you're coming from. Believe me, I know all about nicknames, but what do you want me to call you?"

He knew what he wanted, but was afraid the truth would tell more than he wished to reveal about his state of mind. "I don't know. What do you prefer?"

"I knew you as Adam first."

There was no use concealing his smile. "Adam it is. Oh, and I need your help."

She raised her eyebrows. "With?"

"Portia brought a friend for me to meet. I

wanted to let her down easy, so I told her I'd been looking forward to seeing you. It's not an outright lie, but I let her believe there might be more between us."

Her head tilted up then down. "Oh, I see. Trying the *Cute Cousin's Coming Fake*. You steal that from Brad's playbook?"

He chuckled. "You're speaking my language." *And it's captivating.* "Actually, he told me to use it if she turned out to be a dog."

"I can't believe Portia brought you a dawg. That's how we say it down here." She brushed mascara on her lashes.

"She's not a dawg." He grinned. "I'm from Mississippi, so I can turn it on if need be. She's just…not for me."

"I'm the lucky one then." She wriggled her eyebrows. "Let me finish getting fixed up, so I don't embarrass you."

He returned to the party and let the smile he felt inside show on his face. It'd seemed like a long time since he had a reason to smile. Christmas was looking brighter.

CHAPTER TWO

Eva took a deep breath before she joined the party guests. She'd avoided social situations for almost two years. When her husband Mickey was alive, she was great at parties. Since his death, she stuck to the necessities: gym, work, groceries, home.

Sweat trickled down her back as she entered the main room, and she let her fingers glide across her wet palms. She went straight to the kitchen island, which held an assortment of finger foods, looking for a napkin to dry her hands.

"Here you go, Eva. Brad got your favorite beer." Portia handed her a bottle. "Do you want a koozie?"

"Um, no thanks." Eva opened the fridge and exchanged the beer for a water. She hadn't told Brad she'd given up drinking.

When she closed the door, she screamed and jumped, eventually settling her hand on her heart to calm it down.

Adam laughed. "Do you scare easily?"

"I'm not used to refrigerator-sized men sneaking up on me. I think I peed a little."

"If you can dish out the size jokes, I'm sure you can take them too, right?" His midnight blue eyes sparkled under the fluorescents.

"I'm a good sport, but I'll try not to mention it again if it bothers you." Her wet palms made it impossible to open the plastic cap.

He took the bottle from her and opened it effortlessly. "Not enough strength in those tiny hands of yours."

She looked down at her palms. Mickey always said she had big hands, but he hadn't been a large man. She held up a hand, and Adam put his palm against hers. It was like an elf next to Santa. It was nice to have something tiny. "I'll have to keep you around for the jobs I can't *hand*le."

His laughter reverberated through her, resulting in a tingly feeling in her chest.

Portia interrupted their moment by tugging Eva's arm. "Come meet my friend, Amy."

Eva looked over her shoulder, hoping Adam would come, but he turned the other way. Amy must've been the woman he wasn't interested in.

Eva was admiring his physique when she tripped over the coffee table. "Son of a fruitcake, did you see that?" She winced and gripped her knee, which felt as if the tendon had been severed by the wooden corner. "That thing jumped out in front of me."

It was then she realized she was wearing Portia's martini.

"Let me see." Brad knelt in front of her. "It's merely a flesh wound." His British accent was for crap, but Portia laughed like he was Prince Harry.

He did kind of favor the royal, but Brad was bigger. He'd played college ball, and fifteen years later, he still had the bulk he'd put on in school.

"I'll be all right in a minute. Can I sit there?" Eva motioned to an empty spot on the couch.

The man seated next to her turned out to be Brad's employee, Jimbo. She'd heard a thousand tales about the man who sported blondish hair to contrast his thick dark, red beard.

Brad owned an environmental company and was an engineer. Jimbo was his lead field man who spent hours in his favorite place, the great outdoors, taking water, soil, or air samples for their clients. The best part was nothing appropriate ever came out of Jimbo's mouth. They might have been kindreds because she thought the things he said, but wasn't brave enough to let them past her lips most of the time.

Eva grew up in a small Georgia town and knew her share of rednecks. Heck, she was one when she needed to be. Like Adam, she could turn it on, but Jimbo was like all the members of the Redneck Comedy tour rolled into one.

When her stomach hurt from laughing and her butt hurt from clenching to hold in the flatulence her girdle was trying to squeeze out of her, she excused herself to the powder room. She almost called it a night and crawled into bed, but settled for taking her contacts out to give her tired eyes a break.

The martini spill was drying and barely noticeable on the dark fabric, but her dress smelled like vermouth. She shimmied out of her spandex undergarment and hoped everyone was drunk enough not to notice her pooch that no amount of abdominal work would melt.

She sucked in her belly as much as possible as she made her way back to the living room.

Amy had Adam cornered. When Portia spotted Eva, she headed her way to run interference. It was clear Portia had plans for her friend, and Eva had too many miles on her to put up with childish games..

She made an about-face and returned to her room.

***

Adam sat up in bed and struggled to open his eyes. Someone was knocking. It sounded again, but it wasn't on his door. He looked to the curtain's edge where pale morning light was beginning to glow. He growled as he rolled out of bed and into sweats and a T.

He opened the door to his bedroom, and Amy fell in. She and Portia both squealed, and he didn't find it nearly as charming as he had Eva's fright the previous evening. He not being a morning person might've had something to do with it.

"Sorry to wake you." Portia leaned her ear against Eva's door. "I can't find Brad. He might be in there."

It was then they heard laughter and a dog yip from the living area. The trio went down the hall to find Brad, Eva, and Bella entering the back door.

"There you are. I was worried to death." Portia tried to hug Brad while he struggled to get out of a heavy winter coat.

She let out a howl. "You're freezing."

Adam squeezed his temples.

"Yeah, the temperature dropped last night. It's mid-twenties, and there's frost everywhere."

"Why are y'all up so early?" Portia hugged herself and rubbed her arms.

"We've got a busy day." Brad hung his coat on the rack by the door. "Family stuff. I'll take you home…unless Amy can take you."

"Sure." Amy looked less attractive in the

morning light with smudged makeup. "Can I get a cup of coffee first?"

Brad disappeared into his room. Adam wanted nothing more than to go back to bed, but as Eva struggled with the coffee pot, he felt compelled to help. "Let me."

She smiled and moved back to give him space. She looked remarkably good for the ungodly hour of seven a.m. Her eyes and cheeks were bright from the cold, and she wore a green and tan crocheted stocking cap on her head. His ex wouldn't have been caught dead in one of those, which made him like it even more.

"Hey, Eva." Portia pushed Bella away. "Brad tells me you work for a dentist. Amy is a dental assistant."

Eva bent to give the dog a vigorous pet, starting at her ears all the way to her furry rump. Bella actually looked like she was smiling.

"I don't work in the office. It's a husband and wife dental team, and I take care of things on the domestic front."

"You're a housekeeper?" Amy's lip curled.

"Yeah, but I also keep the kids in clean diapers and keep them from running into the street or the ocean."

"So, you're a nanny?" Portia asked.

Adam watched Eva nod before he added the coffee grounds. Brad had a way of giving enough information to be misleading, but she'd told Adam she took care of kids during one of their phone conversations.

Her hand landed on his arm. "Do you need a filter?"

"Son of a…" He stopped short of swearing.

"Snowflake." She finished for him.

"I'm not awake yet. Maybe I should let you take over."

She took the basket and dumped the grounds into the trash, which Bella found very interesting. "Back that snout up, pup."

Adam bent and distracted the dog with a scratch behind her ears.

"I heard your husband died." Amy plopped onto a bar stool. "I wish my ex would die."

Eva dropped the basket in the sink, and Adam's first instinct was to tackle Amy and "accidently" step on her neck as he got back to his feet. Somehow, he thought the callous woman would like the tackling part. His next reaction was to offer Eva comfort, but she was placing the coffee filter and adding grounds, so he turned inward.

"I wish my ex would take me back." Adam didn't know where the words came from, but with all eyes on him, he knew he'd said it aloud.

"Well, if she's still alive, at least you have a chance." Eva pressed the start button on the machine and turned for the coat rack. "Hey,

Brad, time to unload."

She put her coat on and went out the front door. Brad came out of his room and followed her.

When the door closed, Amy said, "Is it just me, or is she kind of bitchy?"

"I don't think she likes me, and Brad cares about what she thinks." Portia rubbed her arms against the cold blast of air, which had entered the house.

Adam didn't want to spend another minute around either woman, so he headed for the shower.

As the hot water streamed down his back, he tried to figure out if he still really wanted Renee back. He asked himself, "If she showed up today and begged for another chance, would I do it?"

For the first time in eleven months, he wavered a little, but the answer was still yes.

CHAPTER THREE

Eva climbed onto the second highest rung of the ladder to place the final wreath on the front of Brad's house. Smaller wreaths centered the top of each of the four big windows. Pine boughs brightened with large red ribbons would look elegant under the outdoor spotlights she had yet to set up.

Decorating was a hobby left over from her days of working in a floral and gift shop. She'd learned to wrap with precision and make bows like nobody's business. Since she had to get all the decorating done before the family came over late in the afternoon, she'd done a lot of prep work beforehand, which is why the back of her Honda SUV looked like she'd raided Mrs. Clause's storage closet. Some of the decor came from her own supply, but others were hand-me-downs and leftovers from the decorating jobs she'd done on the side to make extra money. Her employers had a lot of friends who wanted the classy Christmas vibe and were capable of paying top dollar for it.

Brad had offered to pay her to do his house, and she'd tried to kick him. He didn't know her financial situation and was trying to be helpful. But he was family, more like a brother than a cousin, and she'd been offended.

She was actually doing okay because fear kept her from overspending. In the year and nine months since she'd become a widow, she'd stuck to the basics for survival: shelter, food, and gas to get to work.

Mickey had been generous with his income, often saying she shouldn't have to want for anything. He hadn't left her in a tight spot. But she'd never gone to college, never liked school, and knew she'd never make millions being a nanny, decorator, and yoga teacher. The money didn't matter too much because she enjoyed the work and could support herself if she was careful.

She straightened the bow and leaned back a little, making sure the wreath was centered. Starting down the ladder, the knee she'd hit the night before hollered at her. She let go with one hand to rub the offending limb about the same time a deep voice urged her to be careful. She fell, flapping her arms as if they might turn into wings.

Adam caught her like she was covered in pig

skin, and she only elbowed him in the side of the head once. Solid arms pulled her against a chest made of concrete. It would've hurt more if he weren't in a down jacket. She was thankful to the geese who'd lost their feathers.

"I've got you." He settled her feet on the ground, but held on to steady her.

She reached up to touch his head. "I'm so sorry I hit you."

"You call that a hit?" His white teeth reflected the sun.

"Yeah, I do—an elf hit. I think I'm jinxed this Christmas. I hope I don't wind up in the hospital before it's over." She tested the sore knee. It was fine as long as she didn't bend it too much.

"Do we need to put you in a helmet and practice pads?" His smile crinkled the corners of his eyes.

"That might not be a bad idea. I think I'm done with the climbing for today."

No sooner had the words left her mouth, than Brad pulled up with a tree longer than his crew cab truck. "Check it out. Ain't she a beauty?" He opened the passenger door, and Bella jumped out.

"Did you get the biggest one on the lot?" she asked.

"Yep." Brad bounced like a little boy. "The wreaths look great."

"Thanks." She limped to her SUV and held up a spotlight. "They'll look good at night, too."

"Cool. Yo, Mack, can I get a little help with this tree?"

"Sure thing. Put me to work." He paused and turned to Eva. "Don't get back on the ladder without one of us with you, okay?"

She saluted him and then felt terrible for doing it. She used to salute Mickey when he'd pretended to order her around, but he was in the Navy, so it was apropos.

How did a girl salute a professional football player? A touchdown dance? The Heisman pose?

The guys disappeared inside with the tree, so she practiced the pose as she placed spotlights along the ground. On the third try, her knee reminded her she shouldn't bend that way.

***

Adam lifted the tree while Brad slid the base underneath and secured it. Bella tried to drink the tree water, and Brad had to keep shooing her away.

"Brad, I heard what you told Portia this morning about family stuff today. If you want me to make myself scarce, just say the word."

"Are you kidding? You *are* family, and I just wanted her gone. She was getting on my nerves. I couldn't even sleep in my own bed last night because after I cleaned up the party *she* wanted to have, she and Amy were passed out in it." He wrapped his arms around his dog. "Bella was more upset about it than I was, weren't you, precious? We had to sleep on the couch."

"Sorry, man. You should've knocked on my door." He bent to scratch Bella's ears. "I would've let this pretty girl sleep with me."

"Ha, thanks a lot. Eva would've let us in, too, but I knew she was tired from her drive. I felt bad about letting Portia talk me into a party on the night she got here. It was hard enough for her to come without adding additional stress."

Adam stood back to examine at the tree. "She seems okay to me."

"You should've met her before. She was a life force, drew people into her orbit."

They looked at the front door when it opened.

Eva pulled her gloves off as she admired the tree. "I hope we have enough lights."

"I bought extra." Brad dashed to his room.

Adam looked after him. "I'm not sure I've ever seen him so excited."

"The Greene's are big on Christmas. It'll rub off, and soon you'll be sprinting for the ornaments."

"If I could still sprint, I'd be recovering from a big game and enjoying a bye week."

"I'm sorry, Adam. I didn't mean to bring up a

bad subject."

He ran his hand through his hair. "Ah, it's not your fault. It's life. My year sucked, but I'm thinking it can only get better from here. I just have to figure out what to do now."

"You could have a career catching ladies who fall off ladders." She grinned.

"You scared me to death. I'm glad I was there."

"Me too." She pulled garland out of a box. "I don't want to overstep, but the military has career counselors who help people when they're getting out and transitioning to civilian life."

What she suggested was a good idea. He might've thought of it eventually.

Brad returned with lights, and Eva directed them to start on the tree while she decorated the mantle with garland, lights, bows, and pine-scented candles.

Adam closed his eyes and inhaled the smell of Christmas. It took him back to his childhood when the holidays had been simple and filled with love. It had been enough, even if he'd gotten fewer gifts than many of his friends.

His parents were both gone now, leaving him alone in the world. He'd always missed them at Christmas, but this year was worse because Renee and her family had divorced him.

"Eva, will it make you sad if we put on *Christmas Vacation*?" Brad asked from his side of the tree.

Adam wanted to kick himself for his self-pity when a young widow sat a few feet away, humming "Silent Night". According to Brad, after her husband's plane was shot down, she'd spent that first Christmas isolated from friends and family. This would be her second, and everyone was concerned about how she'd handle it.

"It's tradition." Eva's hands were filled with red ribbon, which looked like half of a huge bow. "Let's see if I can remember all the lines."

His mom always told him women were the stronger sex. Adam had never really believed it, until he looked hard at Eva.

She didn't pretend not to feel her loss, but she seemed determined not to let it drag her into a pit she couldn't get out of.

He could take a page from her playbook.

CHAPTER FOUR

The final bow was hung, and Eva smelled like pine sap and road slime. The shower called her name, and she closed herself in the bathroom when the caterers arrived to set up. Brad claimed he wanted to host a big family party to celebrate his first Christmas in his new house, but Eva suspected it was for her.

When she shaved her legs, she groaned at the bruise, which had decided to show up on her knee. So much for the short party dress she'd planned to wear. She took pain medicine before she showered, but by the time she was dressed, her joint throbbed.

She limped into the living room and found Adam on the couch, watching college football.

"Where's Brad?"

"Shower."

"Reindeer poop." She sat in the armchair and rubbed her knee.

Adam knelt in front of her and took her bare

ankle in his hands. His warm, tender touch replaced the ache in her knee with a need low in her belly. She sucked in a breath and his gaze met hers. She looked down and tried not to hyperventilate as he lifted the hem of her calf-length skirt.

"Nicely done, little one. I've got something that'll help." He went down the hall and returned a moment later with a bottle of ointment. "Lean back, I'll *hand*le this." He flexed his fingers.

She'd started it, so she did as asked. The smell of mint and rosemary filled the air as she watched him massage the lotion from mid-calf to low-thigh. Getting doctored had never felt so good.

"Those giant paws of yours are magic."

"Just call me Santa Paws." He wriggled his eyebrows.

"Only if you wear one of the Santa hats I brought." She was outright flirting like a fan-girl.

One corner of his mouth turned up. "I'd look ridiculous."

"So? It's fun to look ridiculous."

He dropped the pretense of a smile. "I'm pretty sure you'd make a Santa hat look sexy."

Her eyebrows shot up.

He blushed and looked down as he capped the medicine bottle. "I'm sorry. I shouldn't have said that."

She put her hand on his retreating arm. "I'm glad you did. It's nice to know I haven't completely lost it."

He cleared his throat. "No, you haven't."

She stared into his midnight blue eyes and swallowed hard. She wanted to return the compliment, but words failed her. Instead, she felt herself being drawn in, leaning toward him. Her eyes landed on his lips when he licked them. A few more inches and she could have them.

The front door opened. "Aunt Eva."

She blinked to release herself from the trance Adam put her under before turning toward her second cousins who raced to her side. "Oh, my goodness, who's been feeding you guys fertilizer? Remember our deal? You can't get taller than me."

They took turns hugging her.

"I'm already taller than you, Auntie." Twelve-year-old Zach was gangly and on the verge of a voice change.

She faked a tear. "You used to love me." She looked to Adam. "The kids were the only ones who made me feel tall, growing up in the land of the giants."

Six-year-old Savannah patted Eva's head. "I still love you."

"Y'all move over, so I can give my baby girl

a kiss." The deep, gruff voice was like salve to her wounded soul.

Eva blinked back tears and stood to embrace the uncle who'd taken her in when his sister, her mom, had abandoned her. His red hair was almost white now.

Aunt Lynn reached out to hug her. "The house looks beautiful. You even decorated the dog."

Bella pranced around in a Holly Berry neck bandanna.

"I had help from a couple of over-sized elves." Eva winked at Adam.

"I'm glad you put those boys to work," Aunt Lynn said. "The toy soldiers guarding the front door are very Brad. You managed to make it festive without it being too feminine."

"Thanks. He was starting to complain about all the red bows until I got those out."

"Eva, we forgot to hang the mistletoe." Brad raised his voice from the kitchen. "Leave it to the newlyweds to notice."

Eva hugged the rest of the family. Brad was the youngest of three boys, and she was five years younger than him. When Eva went to live with them, the oldest boys had already been in college. The second of them had married earlier in the year, and Eva had never met his very pregnant wife.

When everyone sat down to dinner, Eva tried

very hard not to look for Mickey. He always went last in the food line, and therefore, usually wound up sitting somewhere other than by her side.

Aunt Lynn sat next to her and took her hand. "We're so glad you came. I've missed you."

"We all have." Uncle Charlie lifted his glass. "To our Eva. May this be the best Christmas ever."

She swiped a tear from her cheek. He always made the same toast, except this time he added the part with her name. She looked around the table at everyone wearing the different variations of Santa hats she'd brought: red, pink, green, striped, and camo. Even Adam sported a red one with white fur trim and said it was better than wearing a helmet.

Mickey would be proud she was with her family. He loved being with them, and he wouldn't have wanted her to put the distance she had between them. They were the family who kept loving her, even when she had nothing to give them in return.

***

Adam didn't feel like an outsider at the Greene's family dinner. In fact, he felt more welcome than he ever had with Renee's family. In comparison, her family had seemed a little disingenuous, like they were trying hard to impress him, and they thought ostentatiousness was the way to win him over. He often left feeling like no one had been real with him, his wife included.

He was just a man and wanted people to treat him like he was normal. The assumption that professional athletes gloried in the applause wasn't true in his case.

The Greenes treated him like one of their own—from Eva putting him to work decorating, to Brad's mom forcing him to eat one more bite of vegetables before he could have dessert.

Something dawned on him. Why did he miss Renee when he didn't really like her that much?

Maybe it was because he hated to lose.

When it was time to clear the table, he went to Eva and took the plates from her hand. "You need to sit."

"But I…"

He placed the plates on the table, picked her up and carried her to Brad's recliner.

"But, Santa Paws, it feels much better." Her wide-eyed innocent look made her appear younger than her years.

He shook his head. "You need RICE."

"I'm too full for rice." She put her hands on her abdomen.

"Rest. Ice. Compression. Elevation." He tilted the lever on the chair to lean her back.

The family went on about their business

while he ventured to the freezer. He grabbed a tea towel and returned to place a bag of frozen corn on her knee. Then he went to her room and got a pillow from the bed to prop under her leg and get it a little higher.

"How do you know to do all this?" she asked.

"Two knee surgeries and more sprains, bruises, and pulled muscles than I can count."

"That's a tough line of work. I'm glad you're moving on."

He smirked while she squirmed and settled. "Will you be needing anything else?"

"Only this." Somehow, from a nearly laid out position, she managed to pull the Heisman pose, using the corn in place of the ball.

He'd never fallen down laughing before, but he grabbed his gut and took a knee. "You're too much."

Once recovered, he nudged Lynn over at the sink. He rinsed dishes while she washed.

She pressed her elbow into him. "Thank you."

"It's not a problem. I've washed my share of dishes."

"No, I mean…" She looked over her shoulder. "To hear her laugh…after everything."

Adam nodded.

"It's amazing she turned out as well as she

did." Lynn passed him a plate.

"You're not just talking about her husband's death."

"No, but I thought that might be the final blow to knock the wind out of her sails." She lowered her voice. "When we got her, she'd been taking care of herself for awhile. Her mother was missing three days before Eva told someone, but in Eva's defense, the woman kept odd hours and was rarely home, except to sleep during the day. It was after Eva realized her mom hadn't been home for several days that she started looking for her."

"What happened to her mom?"

"After an investigation, they discovered she'd run away with a patron of the strip club she worked at. When they found her, she told them Charlie could have custody. He'd already gone down there and was staying with Eva in their dumpy little apartment."

"How old was she?"

"Twelve. She gave us a lot of trouble at first, rebelling and running away. Thankfully, we figured out she was testing us. She'd been good for her mom and still got left behind. She tried a different approach with us, and eventually, she decided the rules and structure meant we cared."

Adam didn't know what to say, but he hadn't imagined the quiet strength he saw in Eva. He already admired her, but the warm feeling growing in his chest was something he was afraid to name. His respect was already deeper than what he'd felt for his wife.

Brad sidled up next to him. "What are y'all doing? I have a dishwasher."

"We're almost finished, honey." Lynn looked around Adam. "Grab a towel and start drying."

Brad mumbled under his breath as he dried dishes.

When they had everything put away, Adam checked on Eva. Bella had joined her in the recliner, and he was a little jealous of the dog.

"Hey, Mack, you made any career decisions yet?" Charlie asked while he tuned his guitar.

"Not yet."

"We can brainstorm with you." Charlie made up a song on the spot to the tune of "Joy to the World". "You could be a sports announcer…" The list went on and on, from a spokesperson for arthritis cream to a used car salesman.

He was seated on the floor next to Eva's chair, and when the song was over, she looked inside the back collar of his shirt.

"Do you have a hard time finding clothes to fit your twenty-inch neck?"

His face got hot. "It's not twenty inches."

"You're not even legal with that neck. You can go bigger. More shoulder shrugs at the gym ought to do it." She winked.

"If you must know, yes. Sometimes, it's hard to find clothes to fit right."

"You could do a clothing line for big and tall men. Call it Big Mack's, but don't let McDonald's sue you." She swept her hand in front of her face. "I can see it now, an athletic line, casual, formal. You should think about it."

"I know nothing about designing clothes."

"You hire the designer, approve the fabric, colors, styles. Model them yourself for advertising, kinda like Jessica Simpson and those folks."

He propped his elbow on his knee and gripped his chin. It was a realistic suggestion, and one he'd never entertained. He wanted to kiss Eva for sharing it with him until he remembered Renee. She would love the idea. It might be a venture she could help him with, and it might bring her back to him.

He asked himself the question again.

CHAPTER FIVE

Eva stood between Adam and Brad at church Sunday morning. At five-three, she felt like a hobbit, so she was determined to look for elf ears and shoes while shopping with the girls after lunch.

It was the Sunday before Christmas. A family of four lit the fourth candle of Advent while a young woman sang a ballad-style arrangement of "Angels We Have Heard on High".

Eva tapped Brad with the back of a finger. "She's pretty. Is she single?"

"Don't know her." He tilted his head and raised one eyebrow. "Don't go trying to fix me up at church."

"You'll find a nicer woman at church than you will at happy hour."

"Says the girl who met her husband at a strip club."

Adam leaned in. "What?"

"I wasn't working there." She punched Brad's thigh before she leaned to whisper to Adam. "I was with a bachelorette party, and he asked me for a lap dance."

"Did you give it to him?"

"Not that night."

Brad thumped her arm hard.

She grabbed the injured appendage. "Ow."

"Kids." Eva froze as Uncle Charlie's hand landed on her shoulder, and she pressed her lips tight to hold in a giggle.

Brad stuck his tongue out at her just before his dad's other hand landed on his shoulder. Eva grinned.

"You're in trouble," Adam whispered close to her ear.

His hot breath tickled her neck and sent a chill racing along her skin. She squeezed her hands into fists, fighting a sudden urge to reach over and hold his hand. He was trouble, making her feel womanly things during church.

Eva sought out the soloist after the service, and once they'd talked for a few minutes, she called Brad over. "Meet Andrea. I told her how much we enjoyed her song. She's a geologist who works for the state."

"Really?" Brad practically elbowed Eva out of the way as he moved in to talk science.

Eva backed up and bumped into an immovable object. It had to be Adam. She turned and grinned.

"Don't you think Portia might be a little miffed to know you're trying to set Brad up with another woman?"

Eva grimaced. "I honestly forgot about her. Maybe Brad will too."

"You really don't like her?"

"Do you?"

"Not really, she reminds me of..." He stopped and looked away.

She tugged on his sleeve. "Of who?"

"No one. My point is, I think she's trying too hard to be who she thinks others want her to be."

"I think she's trying to hook a rich husband. She asked me how much money engineers make." Eva glanced to see Brad still engaged in conversation with Andrea.

"What did you tell her?"

She shrugged. "I have no idea, but I gave her a breakdown of the pay scale for Naval officers, and her eyes glazed over."

Adam put his hand on her arm. "That reminds me. Brad's really worried about how you're doing money-wise. He gave his mom cash for when you guys go shopping later."

Out of nowhere, emotions welled up, and she covered her face with her hands to hide a sob.

Adam pulled her into his chest, tucking her

under one arm and rubbing her back with the other. "I didn't mean to upset you. I just didn't want you to be mad at him. He wants to help, and he doesn't know how."

She wiped under her eyes with her knuckles and exhaled a shaky breath. "I'm not mad. That's really thoughtful, but I'm okay. At least with money, and one day, I might be okay otherwise."

He took her chin in his hand. "You're already better than okay. You don't even know your own strength, but it's beautiful. You're beautiful."

She wanted to kiss him like crazy, right there in the church parking lot. Just lift up on her tiptoes and lay one on him. She flattened her palms against his chest and took a deep breath.

"Andrea's gonna join us for lunch." Brad, who now stood right beside them, tilted his head to look first at Adam, then at her. "Oh, my God, are you okay?"

Eva laughed and dropped her chin until her forehead rested on Adam's chest, his arms still wrapped tight around her. "I'm better than okay."

"Well, the preacher is looking over here."

Adam's hands loosened and slid down until he no longer held onto her.

She lifted her head and stepped back. "It's not what you think."

"I know, but what will other people think?"

"Who am I here to impress?" She put her hands on her hips.

"G-God," Brad answered.

"Do I need to explain anything to Him?"

"No, He knows your heart."

"Thanks for clearing that up for me." Eva tried not to laugh.

"You stinker, I'm gonna tell Bella to bite you when we get home." Brad put her in a headlock and gave her a noogie.

"Santa's gonna bring you switches." She squirmed to get away.

"Kids."

Eva and Brad straightened, turned to face Uncle Charlie, and spoke in unison. "Sorry, Charlie."

As they left for lunch, Eva leaned back in the seat. She'd made it through the service without Mickey consuming her thoughts, but she wasn't sure if that was a good thing. Was it too soon to let him go?

***

Adam opened his eyes and wished the dream was real. Something about Eva screaming his name filled the empty spot in his chest. He recognized her voice, not to mention she was the only person who called him by his real name.

The doorbell rang like a fire alarm, and then,

not two seconds later, it sounded again. He bolted out of bed and rushed to the front door. He flung the door open and stepped out under the alcove.

Eva chased Bella, who ran and jumped around the front yard. "Help me. She's not wearing her collar."

He bent down. "Bella, come here."

The dog ran straight to him, and he put an arm around her.

Eva ran up and leaned over, resting her hands her on thighs while she panted. "She ran out while I was looking for the paper, and I chased her down the street and back, and all around the yard. You must sleep like a log because every time I ran by your bedroom window, I yelled for you." She took a few deep breaths. "I thought she was gonna get run over or lost with no name tag."

"She probably liked being chased." He patted Bella's head. "Most girls do."

He was waiting for Eva's response when the dog's cold, wet nose investigated his inner thigh, stopping short of his festive boxers.

"Can you get her? I'm not exactly dressed for the occasion." The red flannel shorts had the word *HO* stamped all over them.

Eva crossed her arms over her chest and smirked with her head tilted to one side. "No, I'm too tired from the chase."

He guided Bella inside before he stood and faced Eva. Electricity sizzled between them in the frigid morning air.

She took a step toward him, eyes roaming from his waist, pausing on his chest, and up to his eyes. She didn't hold his gaze though.

She looked down as her cheeks flushed with more color. "I better go find her collar."

He backed against the cold brick exterior and gestured for her to go in. Once inside, he closed the door and leaned against it, trying to decipher what had just passed between them. He was rusty, but he could swear he saw desire in her bright green eyes.

As he walked down the hall to his room, he glanced over his shoulder to see Eva staring after him with a small smile on her dark pink lips.

He turned around with a grin. "Did you get your eyes full?"

"I've seen enough for now." She squeezed her eyes shut and shook her head. "Wow. You're really something."

He bit the inside of his cheeks to not smile. "Something good?"

She nodded several times. "I've never seen so many muscles, and I work at a gym."

"You do?"

"Well, I just teach a morning yoga class. Not many weight lifters come, but they should."

"I love yoga." *What was he saying?* "Let me rephrase. I'm terrible at it, but I like to challenge myself."

She walked over to the kitchen counter. "Brad left us guest passes for the gym, and they have a yoga class. You wanna go with me?"

The idea of seeing her in tights, bent into a pretzel shape, appealed to his desire, but it wouldn't be good for his vanity. He wanted her to see him being good at something.

"I'll do your workout with you, if you do mine with me after. It's back day."

A big smile spread across her face. "I've got your back."

His heart actually changed rhythm. "I'll go get dressed."

"Yeah, the people at the gym don't care for half-naked exercisers."

As it turned out, the gym was fairly deserted. Adam assumed it was due to Christmas vacation and schools being closed. The yoga class had four students, including him and Eva. He couldn't keep his eyes off of her. She had long lines for a short person, and she made it look so easy.

"I didn't know elves were so good at yoga."

She cut her eyes up at him. "Santa Paws is jealous because he can barely touch his toes." She stopped and put a hand on his arm. "In all seriousness though, you did very well."

"Maybe you can help me with my downward facing dog later."

"Yeah, you, me, and Bella can all practice together." On the way out of the group fitness room, she stopped. "Hey, there's your next career. You can make yoga videos for big dudes. Call it NFL- New Found Length."

"Or No Flexibility Left."

"Or Never Felt Loose." She snorted and covered her mouth.

He laughed, enjoying their easy banter. She could take a sore subject and make him smile about it.

She was a good sport with his workout routine. He liked the way she grunted out the last couple of reps. Renee had never worked out with him.

Come to think of it, they really didn't have much in common, except for football and when that was gone, so was she. She'd been a cheerleader when they met, but she quit after they married.

He was aggravated with himself for always thinking of her. She'd done him wrong, and he should be mad. He'd let himself be hurt, but never angry.

He moved the pin down to the lowest plate in the stack and took his anger out on the machine.

"Whoa, you stay that mad, and your back's

gonna kill you later."

He let the V-bar go and the plates dropped with a bang. "How do you know I'm mad?"

Her eyes looked up at the ceiling as she shrugged slowly. "I know we just met, but I feel like I know you. I saw your face change from pleasant to hurt to mad, and it really makes me want to kick her booty."

Anger faded to laughter. "You could totally take her, even though she has a few inches on you."

"We Southern elves don't fight fair." She put up her fists.

Words flew from his mouth before he could even think to reverse them. "I have the biggest crush on you."

CHAPTER SIX

Eva backed up and tripped over a weight bench, tipping it over as she went down hard on her tail bone. Just when her knee was improving. "Stuffed stockings!"

Adam lifted her to her feet. "Sorry I shocked you like that and then didn't catch you. I guess catching damsels in distress is one career option that is closed. Are you okay?"

She rubbed the sore place and winced, glad there wasn't more of an audience for her clumsiness. "I might not be able to do down-dog for a while."

"I'm sorry." His hand was still on her arm.

"I'm not. I mean…" She looked down and scratched her head, trying to gather her thoughts. "I'm glad you told me. Is it bad that it makes me happy, even though I'm supposed to be a grieving widow?"

"Who says you're supposed to be anything? Since when do you care what anyone thinks?"

"It's not the living I'm concerned about."

His brows furrowed as his hand dropped.

"Would you want your wife to honor you by grieving after your death?" She held his stare.

"My wife didn't honor me or our marriage vows and I'm still alive."

"You picked the wrong—" Eva cut herself off and looked away. "I'm sorry. I didn't mean that."

"No, you're not far off. I chose her based on the wrappings, without considering what was inside, or what I really wanted or needed in a partner."

Eva discretely rubbed her butt and kicked at the overturned bench. "Well, she's just dumb for not seeing how great you are."

"You keep talking like that I'm going to have to kiss you, grieving widow or not."

Oh gosh, she wanted him to kiss her, right there in the gym, throbbing butt-bone and all. What would Mickey say?

"I can see you're thinking it over. When I do kiss you, I don't want either of us to be thinking about them. They're the past. Soon, I hope we'll be able to leave them there." He bent and righted the bench she'd taken out.

They didn't talk on the way back to Brad's house. Eva squirmed from one sit bone to the other, trying to find a comfortable position. There was no comfort in her thoughts either. A whirlwind of emotions spun around inside with none landing long enough for her to make sense of them.

Adam was right next to her. He was warm and real and alive, and from the little she knew of him, he was good. Maybe if she wanted to seriously consider something with him, she should get to know him better.

"What do you miss most about your wife?"

He glanced over before returning his eyes to the road. "Physical intimacy. What about you?"

"Same."

He smiled before he laughed. "I was only kidding a little. You know this morning when you said you'd have my back?"

She nodded.

"I miss knowing someone has my back. First, my team had it, then Renee, and they all dumped me at once."

"That's rough. When you needed her most, she wasn't there."

"But, next to you, I don't feel like I have anything to complain about."

"Don't feel bad for me. We all make choices, and I chose to love Mickey, knowing his job was dangerous, knowing CACO might show up at my door."

"What's CACO?"

"Casualty Assistance—"

He put his hand up. "Say no more. Sorry—"

"Don't be. I'm wounded, not broken, and not as fragile as I used to be. And, I like that you don't walk on eggshells around me."

"I have a tendency to crush eggshells. It's the big feet." He pulled into the driveway, put the Porsche in park, and turned to face her. "Was your answer serious? About what you miss most?"

Her face got hot. "I wasn't kidding, but…" She looked out the window and then back to him. "I miss physical affection too."

"Like," he took her hand and intertwined their fingers, "this."

Her eyes stung with unshed tears.

His other hand cupped her cheek. "I don't like making you cry."

She smiled. "You're not making me cry. It's just…you're very sweet, and for the first time, in a long time, I don't want to hold onto the past so hard."

***

Adam helped Eva out of the car and into the house. He offered to carry her, but she insisted on walking. Something had changed between them since they'd left the house that morning, and Adam was eager to explore the possibilities.

He opened the front door. "How about a soak in the hot tub?"

She suppressed a smile. "It's either that or let

Santa Paws doctor my backside."

The thought stirred his inner caveman, but he was determined to keeps things light as long as humanly possible. Looking at her again, he knew that wouldn't last long.

He sent her to shower with the pain cream, so she could apply it herself. After he'd had his turn under the cold water spray, he came out to find her on the floor in the living room in front of the lit fireplace.

Seeing Eva laying with her arm over Bella, he knew what she needed. It was one of the things he missed about having a partner. They both longed to be held and touched. When you were lonely, a simple hug could feel like a million bucks.

He went to his room for a pillow before he arranged himself on the floor behind her and covered them with a fleece throw.

She snuggled against his chest, and they watched a Christmas movie from their comfy spot on the area rug. He hadn't known how much he missed cuddling until he was there, in the moment, with his arm around her. He inhaled the scent of vanilla on her skin as he closed his eyes to commit it to memory.

"Well, don't y'all look cozy."

Adam opened his eyes to find he'd dozed off. Brad stood over them with his hands on his hips. Bella lifted her head, but then laid it back down.

"Lazy dog. Aren't you gonna get up and greet me?"

Bella didn't budge.

Eva straightened her legs and stretched. "Hey, cuz. What time is it?"

"Lunchtime. And I thought y'all might be bored."

Adam propped his head on his hand. "No, just resting. We had a busy morning, starting with Bella trying to run away." He explained up to the fall at the gym.

Brad kneeled to pet his dog. "You're tripping over everything these days. You're not pregnant, are you?"

"Immaculately with the miracle child…and just in time for Christmas, too." Eva rolled her eyes.

Brad sat back and crossed his legs. "Why didn't you and Mickey have kids?"

"Because God knew what I could handle and what I couldn't." She rubbed her hand down Bella's side.

"You used to say keeping other people's kids was good birth control." Brad took his shoes off.

"It is."

"What about you, Mack?"

"Renee and I couldn't agree. I wanted them, but she didn't want to be pregnant."

Eva turned to look over her shoulder at him, compassion creasing the corners of her eyes. "Her girlish figure was more important?"

He'd never told anyone about the arguments they used to have. Hearing Eva say it out loud proved again how much some people cared about the wrappings.

Eva rolled onto her back and pulled her knees to her chest. He tossed the blanket back and sat up to study the bruise on her knee.

"We talked about trying when Mickey got back from deployment." She put her feet on the floor and adjusted her hips.

Adam tried not to watch her squirm. "So, you do want kids?"

"I should've known this might happen." Brad stood.

"What?" Eva asked.

Brad pointed back and forth between them. "That you two would hit it off and start talking about babies."

"Does it bother you?" She looked to Adam and back to Brad. "That we like each other."

Brad's face held no expression for a second until the corners of his mouth twitched. "You guys are two of my favorite people, and you've had more than your share of hooey recently. I just want you both to be happy, and if you find it with each other, I'll dance at your wedding." Brad did his victory dance as he backed out of the room.

"He's already got us walking down the aisle." Adam rolled onto his stomach and propped on his elbows. "Be afraid, be very afraid."

"You're the one who should probably lace up your running shoes. Uncle Charlie always threatened to throw me a shotgun wedding."

"How 'bout we keep this just between us until it becomes something? I don't want to pressure you, and I certainly don't want your family to."

"Thank you and thanks for laying with me. That was the best nap I've had in a long time."

"It was well earned. Are you feeling your back yet?"

She flexed her back. "A little bit. Does Santa Paws' miracle cream work on muscle soreness too, or do I just have to suck it up?"

His answer was interrupted when Brad came in and dropped a duffel bag by the garage door. "You kids try not to get in too much trouble while I'm gone."

Eva rolled up to sit on one hip. "Where are you going?"

"Jimbo's testing in North Georgia, and the equipment crapped out on him. I'm going up with replacements and am gonna stay to help him finish up so we can both be home by Christmas Eve."

Adam's heart began to beat faster. He'd have two nights alone with Eva.

The doorbell rang, and Bella pranced over to the door. Adam wasn't sure she'd make a very good guard dog because she liked visitors.

He stood and helped Eva to her feet while Brad got the door. Portia stood there with a big wrapped box in her hand.

Adam whispered to Eva. "He didn't think they were exchanging gifts."

She squeezed his arm. "I'll be right back."

Eva left and came back with a small wrapped package, which she discretely placed under the tree.

Brad came in carrying the box, Portia trailing behind. Adam nodded to the tree and gave an eye signal he made up on the spot.

"What are you wearing?" Portia asked Brad, while stiff-arming Bella. "I've never seen you in grungy clothes."

"This is what I wear in the field. Gets dirty out there." Brad wore a flannel button down, Carhartts, and steel-toe boots as he bent by the tree and picked up the small box.

"I like you better in dressy clothes."

"This is me. Take it or leave it." Brad's voice was filled with frustration.

Adam took it as an exit cue and reached for Eva's and his coats. "We'll take Bella out back."

"Amy said to tell you hey," Portia said to his

back.

He pretended not to hear. It was no use being polite and having it mistaken as interest.

The sunny day had warmed a little, so it felt nice to be outside. He threw a tennis ball, and the dog took off.

Eva stood facing the sun with her eyes closed, and a small smile on her lips. "I'm baking Christmas cookies with Aunt Lynn and the kids this afternoon. You wanna come?"

If it was a family affair, he wanted to be there. He'd spent too much time alone. "I'm all about some Christmas cookies. I have a couple more things on my shopping list. Maybe tomorrow we can pick those up and grab lunch."

"Okay. I can cook for us tomorrow night, if you want."

"It's a date." He waited for her reaction.

She wrestled the ball away from Bella and then threw it. "Ooh, a date. I might have to wear my girdle."

CHAPTER SEVEN

Eva settled into the passenger seat of her SUV as Adam took the wheel. It was strange having a man other than Mickey drive her car, but the thought of Bella riding in Adam's luxury rental had made Eva anxious.

Traffic moved swiftly along the crowded metro Atlanta interstate system and to avoid being crushed by an eighteen wheeler, Adam had to hit the brakes and swerve. The movement threw Bella out of the backseat, so she sought comfort in the front, on Adam's legs.

Eva pulled and tugged, but no matter how she tried, she couldn't get the dog out of Adam's lap. She eventually gave up and gave over to laughter. Adam's deep chuckle joined hers, sending a chill across the surface of her skin. Bella smiled over her shoulder at Eva, rubbing it in because she was being held by the big, strong man. It was crazy to be jealous of the pooch.

Whenever Eva realized she was feeling womanly things again, she had to check in with herself. She closed her eyes. *Stop over-thinking everything.*

Upon arrival, Adam was drawn into a game of catch with Zack while Eva went inside to help bake. When it was time to decorate the sugar cookies, Adam settled at the table with the kids to try his hand at it. They were all wearing their Santa hats, and Eva caught herself thinking how cute he'd look in the hat and his HO, HO, HO boxers. The hard work she'd seen him put in at the gym certainly paid off. She could stare at him all day.

"Aunt Eva, come fix a cookie." Savannah started putting stripes on a candy-cane-shaped confection.

Eva sat next to her and chose a star-shaped cookie to work on. "Did you go see Santa last night?"

"She chickened out and wouldn't sit in his lap." Big brother Zack rolled his eyes.

"He is kinda big and hairy, huh?" Eva nudged the little girl so she'd look up.

She nodded her head.

"Uncle Mack is big and hairy, maybe you can practice on him." Zack licked icing from his fingers.

Adam slid red and green oven mitts on his hands. "Santa Paws is always willing to hear

Christmas wishes."

He winked at Eva as Savannah buried her head under Eva's arm.

"Aww, don't be afraid, sweetie. He won't bite."

"Unless you're a cookie." Adam struggled to get the Santa cookie he'd decorated into his mouth with mitts on. He wound up with icing on his nose.

Savannah giggled as she pushed Eva toward Adam. "You go first."

"You want me to sit in Santa Paws' lap first?"

Savannah nodded with a huge smile no one could say no to.

Adam pushed his chair back from the table and opened his arms. "Come here, little girl, and tell Santa Paws what you want for Christmas."

Eva perched on one of his legs, and he wrapped an arm around her. She was getting her lap time after all. *Eat your canine heart out, Bella.*

She sniffed him. "You smell like Santa."

"What does Santa smell like?" Savannah asked.

"Come see for yourself." Eva held out her hand.

Savannah came closer and leaned over Eva to smell.

"What do I smell like?" Adam asked.

"Cookies." Savannah sang the word.

He rubbed his belly. "Yeah, I eat enough cookies at Christmastime to last me all year."

Eva knew what was under his sweater, so she decided she'd decorate a gingerbread man and give him wash-board abs in honor of Santa Paws.

"Now what does this pretty little girl want me to bring her for Christmas?" Adam looked at Eva.

"I want…" She tapped her index finger on her chin while she thought. "Red, sparkly nail polish, and an unlimited supply of peppermint mochas, but you have to take out all the calories. And a special treat for Bella."

"Is that all?"

Eva nodded.

"Are you sure you don't want a new car or some diamonds or a Barbie doll?"

Savannah bounced up and down. "I want one."

"You do?" Adam's eyes were big. "Well, you better climb up here and tell me what else you want. Elf Eva, I need you to write this down for me."

Eva slid out of the way, and Savannah let Adam lift her onto his lap. The little girl counted off six or seven toys she hoped Santa would bring *and* asked for a treat for Bella.

Eva pretended to decorate more cookies, but she kept glancing up at Adam holding Savannah. Until then, Eva had forgotten about wanting kids someday. Since meeting Adam, her body's reactions were getting stronger and the term *biological clock* took on a whole new meaning.

She tried to dismiss it as hormones, but there was more to it than that. Yes her body craved him, but her heart… Well, she wasn't sure what her heart wanted, but it was very warm toward a certain former ball player who entertained a timid little girl.

***

Adam wasn't sure what to do when Savannah's list kept growing, so he interrupted. "Can you think of anything your Aunt Eva might like from Santa?"

"Daddy said she needs a kiss under the mistletoe."

Adam looked at Eva whose head popped up and cheeks turned a pretty shade of pink.

"Savannah, we should write your list for Santa in a letter and send it to the North Pole," he said.

"I don't know how to spell some things. Will you help me?"

"Of course." He rubbed her head with the oven mitt, causing her hair to stand up from static electricity.

Savannah ran to get a pencil and paper while he removed the mitts. Eva held out a cookie for him and his smile grew bigger.

"You're good for my ego." He took the cookie and bit off a leg. "But not my waistline."

"I think you can afford a couple of carbs at Christmas."

"So can you." He held the cookie to her lips, and she bit off the head.

Savannah was back, and she wanted to sit in his lap. "I got extra paper so we can all write a letter to Santa."

Adam helped Savannah write her letter while glancing at Eva who worked on one of her own. She sealed it in a white envelope, and he longed to know what she'd wished for. He wrote his own letter and sealed it, promising everyone he'd make sure Santa got them. Eva kept hers.

Before he and Eva left, he checked with Lynn to find out if there was anything on the kids' lists they weren't getting and added a few of those items to his shopping list. Lynn objected, but what was the point of being an honorary Uncle if you couldn't spoil your nieces and nephews.

On the way back to Brad's house, Eva rode in the backseat with Bella to keep her from getting behind the wheel again.

"You've got over a hundred thousand miles

on this baby." He glanced at her in the rearview mirror.

"Yeah, we rolled over on the drive down, but she's paid for, so we're sticking together for another hundred thou."

Adam could buy her a new car for Christmas, but he dismissed the idea immediately. That offer would land him in hot water…which gave him an idea.

"Hey, how's your bum?"

"A little sore, but not too bad."

"The hot tub will help." He held his breath.

"You're just trying to see me in a bathing suit."

He glanced back and smiled. "Guilty, but I'll let you get in before I come out, so you won't be shy."

He parked her car next to his rental, and before he could unhook his seatbelt, she made a move that surprised him.

She hugged him from behind with one arm, kissed his cheek, and then rested her head on his shoulder. "Thank you for today. You were a hit, and I bet the next Santa Savannah Greene sees will get an earful."

He laid his cheek on the top of her head. "It was my pleasure, especially the part where my favorite elf sat in my lap."

He got the hot tub cranked up while she changed and then he left to give her privacy while she got in. She might not have needed it, but he really wanted to be a good guy, do the right thing, and not pressure her. He did smile to himself when he thought about the mistletoe Brad hung above the hot tub. He'd wait to see if she noticed.

Adam rested his hands on the side of the tub. "Can I get you a drink before I cannonball in?"

She laughed and shook her head. "I gave up drinking indefinitely."

He settled into the seat across from her, his heart beating a little faster. "Why's that?"

"Too many nights looking at my life through the bottom of a wine bottle."

He dropped his gaze to the bubbling water. "Been there, but it was bourbon, instead of wine."

It had been a dark time after everything fell apart, and he was ashamed of himself for going so far. He'd been afraid he couldn't get back. Binge drinking, bribing the pizza delivery guy to pick him up a fifth because he was too trashed to drive, wearing the same clothes for days. The worst stretch had been after Renee came to see him before the divorce was final, and they'd made love. He'd thought it meant they were making up, but she asked for a larger settlement before she left. He'd blamed himself for being a bad husband, too focused on his career. In hindsight, it was the career she married him for and the salary that went with it. Now that she had her half, he hoped she enjoyed it.

Eva's toe nudged his leg. "Since we're not face down in the toilet, I'd say it's a good day."

He took hold of her foot and rested it on his knee as he pressed his thumbs into the arch.

She leaned her head back and sighed. "Forget what I said earlier, this is my new Christmas wish."

"You're easy to please."

"It's the little things in life." A smile played on her lips.

"Your husband was a lucky man."

"Yes, he was." She smirked and closed her eyes.

"Your next one will be too." He held his breath.

Her eyes remained closed. "Yes, he will."

CHAPTER EIGHT

Eva pressed her hand against her stomach to settle the flapping wings inside. Adam had more testosterone than all the boys on the local high school team combined. He was manly, in great shape, sweet, smart, laughed with her and at her, held her hand, spooned her, and massaged places she didn't know needed massaging.

"What was your real Christmas wish?" His deep voice was playful and serious at the same time.

She opened her eyes and spied a bundle of mistletoe. She sent up a silent thank you to Brad and the Christmas elves who'd pre-arranged the whole scene.

She pulled her foot away from him, leaned across the small space toward him, and tipped her chin up. "I'll give you a hint."

His eyes went up, a whisper of a smile on his lips. "Between Savannah's request and this, I'm beginning to think we've been set up."

She couldn't believe she was about to put a move on Adam "Mack" Riggs. He could crush her like a running back, but he wouldn't because she wasn't a large dude in shoulder pads carrying a football. He could also crush her hopes if he refused to kiss her.

"Is that bad?" she swallowed.

"I can't think of anything better."

She was sure it wasn't true, but in the moment, she chose to believe it. She was still halfway to him, and he hadn't moved yet.

"You gonna leave me hanging?"

"Nope."

Before she could prepare herself, he picked her up under her arms and stood. His arms slid around her back and held her to him, her hands instinctively moved around his neck. Wet bodies and warm lips collided for a kiss that made her forget her name and his. It might have turned into an all-night kind of kiss, if Bella hadn't coughed and vomited beside the hot tub.

Adam set Eva's feet on the bench seat. "I'm calling interference."

"I'll check on her." Eva gave him a quick peck, but his hand cupped the back of her head and pulled her in again.

When he broke the kiss and she managed to get a word out between heavy breathing, it was accompanied by a hand gesture. "Time."

She missed the top step climbing out of the tub, so she banged her foot and fell into Adam's arms. "Slippery sleigh-bells." She laughed to keep from crying as more heat flooded her face. "I'd be up snow creek without a jacket if you weren't here to catch me when I fall."

"Two out of three ain't bad." He carried her out of the hot tub and set her feet on the floor where she wrapped a towel around herself before she went about the task of cleaning up dog puke.

She kept pausing to re-secure the towel around her chest. Adam soothed Bella, and of course, the dog seemed fine.

Eva wasn't fine. Her heart wouldn't slow down. Her skin was hot and her mind raced. It had been her first post-Mickey kiss. She never thought she'd have a life after him, much less a kiss.

"Eva."

"Huh?" She blinked.

"I asked if you thought we should call Brad or the vet."

"Oh, ah, Brad for sure. Let's see what he says."

Adam made the call while Eva changed into fleece pajamas, which covered her from neck to ankle. It was a mistake to kiss him, especially in a hot tub wearing only a bathing suit. It had been a great kiss, but it was too soon. She wasn't ready.

She took a deep breath and forced herself from her bedroom. She knelt beside Bella and rubbed her belly, unable to make eye contact with Adam. He disappeared down the hall and came back a few minutes later wearing shorts and a T-shirt.

"Brad said to keep an eye on her and call him if she got sick again. He thinks the kids probably fed her something at his mom's today." He sat cross-legged by the dog's head.

Eva continued to pet the dog whose eyes were getting heavy.

"I'm sorry I scared you."

"What?" Her head jerked up. "No, Adam." She scooted closer until she bumped into his legs and took his hands. "You didn't. I scared myself. I got…overwhelmed. I'm sorry—"

He pressed a finger against her lips. "Don't be." He took her hands and made a T. "Use this whenever you need to and don't ever be sorry."

Her smile stretched her lips, and she reached her arms around his neck to hug him. "Thanks for not rushing the passer."

He chuckled. "I'll try to hold off on the pass rush, but I can't promise not to sack you if you give me the signal."

Her heart did a backflip and landed low in her belly. A little sack time with Adam might be just the thing. But if she couldn't get her head and heart out of the past, it would never work.

***

The next morning, Adam waited on the back porch while Bella did her business. They'd stayed up with her, but she hadn't gotten sick again.

Re-entering the house, he glanced at the now empty couch where Eva had slept in his arms. He'd reluctantly left the comfort of her soft, warm body to take dog duty when Bella stuck her wet nose to his arm.

A white envelope on the coffee table caught his eye. *Santa Paws* was written across the front. He opened it and read the note.

My Christmas wish is:
To forget I'm a widow, if only for a night.
Your Elf,
Eva

He blinked and read it again. Was this the signal? It had to be. His palms started sweating. No pressure. He'd performed under pressure for a bunch of years. He could put his game face on and fulfill her Christmas wish.

The shower turned off down the hall. He checked the clock and grabbed his car keys. The trip was short, and when he returned, the hair dryer was on.

He tapped on the door and held the red cup out.

When the door opened, heat and steam hit

him in the face, but her smile hit him deep inside.

"I removed as many calories as humanly possible."

She took the cup. "Oh, my goodness, I love you." Her already pink cheeks darkened. "I didn't mean... Not like... Oh Christmas fudge, who I am I kidding? You brought me a peppermint mocha. I'll love you forever."

His chest tightened, and he bent to kiss her cheek. Her lips brushed his cheek too, and he wanted to get used to the feeling.

He leaned against the door frame. "What's the game plan?"

"Shopping, lunch, back here to wrap Santa presents for the kiddos, then I'll make dinner."

"Good plan. I've heard you're the best gift wrapper in the family."

"I was professionally trained." She sipped her drink and moaned.

His lips twitched at the sound and he wanted to hear more, preferably in bed later. He hoped she enjoyed him as much.

They spent the morning shopping, and while she chose the perfect "Santa" paper, he sneaked to cosmetics to get her something.

Back at the house, while teaching him to wrap, she explained that family presents couldn't be in the same wrapping paper as Santa presents because the kids would figure it out. It made sense, and he was glad she knew all about it and could guide him through. Renee had always been in charge of gifts, and he was pretty sure she had them professionally wrapped. There were so many ways he'd failed her as a husband. He was about to beat himself up over it again until Eva jumped up.

"Our hats." She ran to the back and returned holding his out to him. She wore hers, plus something extra—elf ears and shoes.

He chuckled. "You know how to make a holiday bright."

"Too much?"

He shook his head. "Just right." He positioned his hat, then tapped his cheek. "Santa Paws needs a peck."

She obliged before she seated herself next to him on the floor. His eyes kept drifting from his task to watch her. She had a spark of life he wanted to be close to.

Renee wouldn't be caught dead wearing elf accessories. He'd been comparing the two women quite a bit, and it was time to stop. He pushed his ex out of his mind and resolved to keep her locked out. The rest of the day and night would be devoted to focusing on the present and forgetting the past.

"Have you ever heard the greeting *Christmas Give*?" he asked.

She shook her head. "No."

"Mama always said it. It's like a greeting, instead of saying *Merry Christmas.* It started as *Gift*, but Southerners evolved it to *Giff* or *Give*."

"Christmas Give." She tested the words. "I like it."

"The idea is to be the first one to say it on Christmas day, and whoever you say it to has to give you a gift."

"You're on, sucka." She rubbed her palms together. "Get ready to give me a present."

"Gladly." He winked.

When the presents were wrapped, Eva stretched. "My back is sore from yesterday."

He spread his fingers and flexed his hands. "I've got you covered."

"Will you put some of your miracle magic stuff on me?"

Will I ever. "Sure. I'll be right back."

She followed him and stood in the doorway of his room. "Can we do it in here?"

"You mean the…" He nearly dropped the bottle.

His throat went dry when she pulled her sweater over her head.

She closed the distance between them. "Adam, it's time to execute the play."

He placed the lotion on the dresser and his hands on her waist. "What's the signal if you want me to stop?"

"I won't need it unless you try to rough the passer."

He brushed the back of his fingers down her cheek. "No rough play, I promise."

"I'll try to be gentle when I tackle you." She grinned.

"Let's see what you've got, Little Elf."

She took his face in her hands and kissed him like there was no ref ready to throw a flag.

They set a record for getting out of their clothes, and a few moments later, he heard the sweetest sound he'd ever heard—his name on her lips. It was the first time a woman ever called him "Adam" in bed.

He pulled back to look at her face. "I think we should run that play again."

She giggled. "Instant replay."

"In…super…slow…motion." He kissed her after each word.

He poured every ounce of energy into making her Christmas wish come true. She was completely unguarded with him, so he let his guard down too.

Afterward, he lay stroking her back. "You're the kind of woman who appreciates the little things, which makes me want to give you the moon."

"I'd be happy if you just moon gazed with me sometime." Her smile melted his heart.

They spent the night in each other's arms,

playing, loving, and making Christmas memories neither of them would forget.

She woke him before dawn with a kiss on his neck. "I want this Christmas to last forever."

Before Adam drifted off again, he told himself he wasn't in love.

He'd always been good at lying to himself.

CHAPTER NINE

Eva awoke to an empty bed and a closed door. She smiled and hugged Adam's pillow closer until an ocean of guilt rose around her, threatening to drown her. She sat up in bed and choked on the sob building in her chest. She'd dishonored the memory of her heroic husband and his sacrifice.

She escaped to the bathroom and turned the shower to the hottest setting she could stand. Only scalding her skin would remove Adam's scent. It had been wonderful, but it had been wrong.

Tears mixed with the water streaming down her face. She rested her head against the cool tile wall and closed her eyes to block out the wonderful memories. The night was everything she'd hoped for. Adam was someone she would never forget.

His throat cleared on the other side of the shower curtain. "Are you trying to wash me out of your hair?"

She took a deep breath and clenched her fists. She'd have to tell him it was a one-time thing. Firming her resolve, she peeked around the curtain.

He wore nothing but a Santa hat and red boxers with a moose tangled in Christmas lights with the words *LIGHTEN UP* over the antlers. His hands rested on his hips and a smile she couldn't fight spread across her face. The guilt evaporated and blended with the rising steam. The heat licking her skin could no longer be attributed to the hot water spray.

"I wonder if Mrs. Claus finds her husband as attractive as I do you?" Her gaze scanned his handsome face.

"Do you make all men feel as good as you do me?"

She shook her head. "You're the lucky one."

"Must be my lucky Christmas."

The about-face of emotions made her dizzy. A silent apology to Mickey escaped her mind before she turned her back to Adam. She looked over her shoulder. "I might've missed a spot. You wanna help me out?"

His grin would've melted Aunt Lynn's divinity candy.

Later, when they'd recovered from mutual exertion, he propped on an elbow to watch her.

His thumb grazed her jaw. "If you could go

anywhere in the world, where would you go?"

She thought for a minute. "There's a resort in the Bahamas called Atlantis. Have you been?"

"No, but I've heard of it."

"I used to take care of some kids who went and told me all about it. They have lots of water slides, and one of them has an almost vertical drop and shoots you in a tube through a shark tank. It sounds so cool."

"We could go." His hand stilled. "After Christmas, for the New Year, or in January. You name the time."

She thought about how much fun it'd be to go someplace like that, especially with Adam, but she still needed to decide what she was doing with the rest of her life.

He gently rocked her head in a nodding motion. "Say yes."

"I'll think about it."

"Are you going to move back here?"

She let out a long breath. "I didn't know I'd missed home so much until I got back."

"So, you might?"

She smiled. "Maybe. Why? Are you gonna move here, too, and be my boyfriend?" She said the last word in a little sing-song while wriggling her eyebrows.

"Yes. You have to help me pick out a house and decorate it."

Her lips parted, but no sound escaped. He

was talking about a future, and she didn't know whether to be thrilled or terrified.

His finger traced her lips. "I made breakfast."

"I hope it's not ruined." They'd been behind closed doors a long time.

"I left it in the warming oven."

"A man who knows how to use a warming oven, you get better and better. I guess I have worked up an appetite."

His look was serious as he caressed her cheek. "You should never have to be hungry for anything."

"If you're implying that I was starved for affection, you're right." She closed her eyes against the image of Mickey which filled her mind.

"Hey," he gripped her chin. "No guilt. No regrets. I'm very happy to help you meet your basic needs. Not just today, but every day." His lips brushed hers lightly. "Let's go eat."

They were getting ready to leave the bedroom, her in a fleece robe teasing him about his Jack Skellington Christmas pajamas, when the garage door rumbled indicating Brad was home.

***

Adam started stress sweating because he didn't know how to handle Brad. He and Eva hadn't discussed whether to share the news of their affair, but he'd rather err on the side of caution, taking her feelings into account.

He stopped by the bathroom to grab the red velvet cap ringed in white fur. If it were up to him, he'd sing it from the rafters, but he'd be Eva's *Secret Santa* for as long as she would have him.

The garage door opened into the kitchen as Adam placed the plates of pecan waffles and deer sausage on the counter. Bella bounded to the door to greet Brad.

"You look like doodoo." Adam reached for silverware. "Hungry?"

"No, I stopped for a greasy drive-through breakfast on the way home. We finally finished the test and packed it in this morning. I need a shower and my bed."

"Mornin', cuz." Eva came into the room dressed in jeans, a red sweater, and bare feet.

The clothes hugged all the curves Adam loved. As soon as the L-word seared his brain, he fumbled the plate he held out to her. No way. He would not fall again. Not after what his ex put him through.

His heart had an impenetrable wall of linemen around it, tackles and guards on alert to block anyone who tried to get too close. Somehow, Eva had pulled a blitz and gotten through the defenses. How could a little woman be such a big threat?

After he recovered the plate, he looked at her again. He had a choice to make. Sheer vulnerability crossed her features and just like that, his mind was made up. She'd already won.

He walked around the kitchen island, which separated them, and drew her into his arms. Her hands slid around his waist, and she looked up at him, biting her lip to hide her smile.

"Hold on." Brad interrupted their moment. "Is this what I think it is?"

They both turned in his direction.

Brad sucked in a deep breath. "Mack and Eva sittin' in a tree…"

Adam's shoulders sagged with relief. His friend didn't appear to be angry.

Eva shook with laughter. "If he said it right, it'd be Adam and Eva."

He grinned and gave her a wink.

"What does this mean?" Brad scratched his chin.

Several responses rolled around in Adam's brain. It was new, and he couldn't decide if labeling it would diminish or solidify the power of his feelings. "It's a very Merry Christmas. Go get some sleep. We'll wake you when it's time to leave for dinner."

Brad did his touchdown dance as he headed down the hall.

Eva rested her head on his chest. "Thanks for handling that. I didn't know what to say."

"You don't have to say anything. Whatever this is, I don't want it to end." He kissed her until the doorbell rang.

"I'll get it." She smacked his rear before she turned for the front door.

His stomach growled, reminding him of the food he might need to re-heat. From his position by the kitchen island, he could hear voices, but couldn't see the door.

When Eva rounded the corner with wide eyes, he knew something was wrong.

"What?" He looked past her at the guest who followed. "Renee?"

CHAPTER TEN

Eva watched as the very beautiful Renee Riggs slid her black trench coat off to reveal a short red spandex number that was doing little to contain her extra-large endowments. Between the long, curled hair and the chest, Eva wasn't sure how the woman's small frame didn't topple over.

"Why are you wearing that silly hat, Mack?" Her bony elbow protruded as she placed a hand on her equally bony hip.

"It's Christmas." He set down the syrup bottle he held. "What are you doing here, Renee?"

"It's not Christmas without you, baby. I missed you. I made a mistake." Her full lips formed a sultry pout.

Eva turned away, unable to look at Adam's face. Those were the words he'd longed to hear from his ex. *His* Christmas wish was coming true. She'd gotten her wish too, but it was over now. For one night, she hadn't missed Mickey. The familiar ache was back, but not as bad as it had once been.

"Eva." Adam caught her at the door to her room.

While he searched for words, she said what she thought he needed to hear. "It's okay. Y'all need to talk, see if you can work it out."

"But, I—"

She put a finger on his lips. "She came all this way. Just hear her out."

She squeezed his arm and pushed him toward the kitchen. She wouldn't have been able to move him if he hadn't wanted to go. He paused and looked over his shoulder, so she smiled and nodded before she went in her room and closed the door.

She concentrated on her hair and makeup while she made plans to go over to Aunt Lynn's and Uncle Charlie's house and make sure everything was ready for Christmas Eve. She could use the time to make the meatballs for their traditional spaghetti dinner.

Her mind fretted over trivial things. Anything to keep her thoughts away from Adam and the possibility he might reconcile with his ex-wife.

She wondered what she'd do if it was Mickey. If he'd cheated and left her for someone else, could she take him back? The answer was yes.

As naive as it made her feel, she believed in forgiveness and second chances. She'd gotten a second chance when Aunt Lynn and Uncle Charlie took her in and third and fourth chances when she defied them and they'd loved her anyway. Every new day was another chance to make a course correction and keep moving forward.

Adam could've been another chance for happiness, but even if he couldn't be hers, he was a chance for her to begin her healing. It had already begun. Being with him reminded her life was still worth living. She'd been moving along with her eyes on the rearview mirror, hoping for a glimpse of Mickey and the love they shared.

She wasn't sure she could let go yet, but she could loosen her grip on the past. She knew what she had to do, but she stared at the screen of her phone for a long time before she called the number.

"Robin, how much notice do you need?"

"None, and I mean this in the most respectful way, but Eva, you're fired."

***

Adam slid into a booth at the Waffle House and waited for Renee to sit. She spent five minutes layering napkins on the seat before she carefully arranged herself on the pile.

"This place is so disgusting." She held the menu by the edge with her thumb and forefinger, presumably so the grease cooties wouldn't get her. "Why couldn't we talk at your friend's house?"

"Because he just got in from work and needed to sleep." The truth was Adam really wanted her out of the house, in case Eva overheard anything which might hurt her. She'd been through enough heartache, and he didn't want to be the cause of any more.

"When you told me where you were spending Christmas, you didn't say there'd be another woman staying there."

He couldn't stop the corner of his mouth from twitching. "Jealous?"

"Yes, actually." Her red manicured nails clicked a rhythm on the tabletop. The movement made the diamond he'd given her sparkle. "Who is she?"

He wondered why he'd never noticed how pretentious Renee came off. She'd always wanted a bigger diamond, a bigger house. Thankfully, he'd kept a tight hold on the purse strings after she proved to be an extravagant spender the first year they were married. In retrospect, that was when she'd changed. The girl he'd married learned to placate and manipulate to get what she wanted from him. She'd never given him anything to complain about, and he'd mistaken that for love.

"Brad's cousin." He refrained from saying Eva had given him the night—and morning of his life. Or comparatively, Eva was much more giving in every way, but then it had probably been his fault Renee was closed off. "Why are you here?"

She tossed her hair over her shoulder. "I want you back, Mack."

"What's changed, Renee? How can I make you happy now when I couldn't before?"

She fought with the napkin dispenser and came away with a torn tissue, which she used to dab her eyes. "I was wrong. I was happy, but things were changing and I got scared. I'm sorry I hurt you."

His heart squeezed. It was what he'd wished for a few days earlier, but things were different now. He looked at his ex-wife with new eyes. "What happened with Arty?"

"He's not you, baby. He's a boy. You're a man, my man." She fluttered her eyelashes while she walked her fingers across the table and covered his hand with hers.

He drew his hand away. "If you won't tell me the truth, I can find out."

She covered her face with her hands, and her shoulders shook. "Arty dumped me for a younger woman. She's practically a teenager."

He should take pleasure in knowing karma

was a witch. Now Renee knew how he'd felt when she traded him in, but he couldn't stand to see her hurting. He moved to sit beside her and gave her a hug. She cried on his shoulder for a few minutes. Amazingly, when she looked up at him, her eyes weren't red, and her makeup wasn't smudged.

He shook his head. "Is there anything about you that's real?"

"Baby, I love you. It's real, you have to believe me."

"I used to believe you, but you're the reason why I think love is a game. You've always played me." He closed his eyes and pressed his fist to his forehead. "I was so stupid, but now that I've experienced real, I can't go back to plastic. Good luck, Renee. I hope you'll find happiness one day."

She called his name as he walked away, but he didn't look back.

CHAPTER ELEVEN

Eva was making meatballs when Brad entered the back door of his mom's house. The kids had been in and out, and Eva thought she'd trained herself to not look at the door when it opened.

"Hey, cuz, where's Mack?" Brad's hand landed on her shoulder.

She kept her eyes down. "Not sure."

"What? You let him get away so soon?"

"Let who get away?" Aunt Lynn came in, wiping her hands on her apron.

Eva elbowed Brad in the ribs. "No one. Brad's daydreaming again."

"Stop dreaming and come cut these tomatoes." His mom passed him a knife. "I need to get off my feet for a few minutes, since I'm gonna be up all night cooking for tomorrow."

"We can help, Mama. Eva will stay up and help you. Won't ya, cuz?"

The ham would bake overnight, and by morning, when it was done, the pies would be ready to go in. Then there were the side dishes. Eva's brain was getting tired just thinking about it.

"Of course I'll help. Go rest, Auntie. We've got this." When she'd gone, Eva turned her glare on Brad. "Extortionist."

"Did you ever stop to think it'd make the family happy to know? They love Mack."

"It was one night. Not forever."

"One night with you was all it took for Mickey to want forever."

She didn't think before she acted. The meatball she'd been forming landed in the middle of Brad's chest. "Shut your damn mouth. Don't ever talk about him like that."

His mouth hung open as he scraped the raw meat mixture off his sweater. "Funny, that's the same thing I said to him when he told me that. He meant it as a compliment and he'd been kidding, but I didn't understand that until later."

She couldn't breathe, so she swiped her hands on a nearby towel on her way to the door. "I've got to get out of here."

Her keys were in her car, so she started driving, no place in particular. She used the bottom of the Candy Cane apron she still wore to wipe her tears.

She'd thought the days of spontaneous,

uncontrollable crying were over. She'd expected Christmas to be tough because the previous year had been almost unbearable, but she thought she'd regained a little control.

When she crossed the state line into South Carolina, she knew where her subconscious was taking her. She could be home by midnight, back to the last place she was whole and happy. She slowed and pulled onto the shoulder. As much as she wanted him to be, Mickey wouldn't be there. She could keep looking to the past, or she could turn the car around and drive toward a new start. Even if it didn't include Adam, she owed it to herself. Mickey wouldn't want her stuck in reverse.

When Brad repeated Mickey's words about forever, it was like his ghost had whispered it in her ear. He'd always teased her, but told her truthfully he'd loved her from the first night they met.

She'd been holding onto the remnants of his love in hopes it would keep her going. The realization that the memory wasn't enough, that she wanted and needed more tangible love scared her.

What if she'd already had her chance at love? What if she found it and then lost it again? Could she survive another loss? The answers would tell her which direction to point her car.

***

Adam didn't want to call Brad's house and wake him, but he wanted Eva to know he'd be back after another stop. He didn't have her number, so he tried to hurry. When he got there, he discovered no one was home.

He called Brad who asked if he'd seen Eva, and Brad filled him in on what had happened. Adam's mind ran through places she could've gone. He was angry with Brad for saying the wrong thing and running her off, and he was angry with himself for not being honest with her before he left with Renee.

He checked her room to find her luggage still there, so he sat on the bed and took a few deep breaths to calm down. She wouldn't have left without saying goodbye. He rubbed the achy spot in his chest. He didn't want it to be over so soon, maybe not ever. But definitely not for the foreseeable future.

He stood and called Brad again. "Where can I look?"

"I don't know. She's not answering her phone. She's probably halfway back to Virginia."

"Her stuff is here."

"Doesn't matter." Brad's voice held no hope.

"Give me her number."

Adam dialed and heard the ringing in her room. He lifted the pillow and found her phone, his heart sinking. Every horrible thing he could imagine happening to her ran through his mind in a matter of seconds.

He squeezed the phone until the plastic cracked. "Dammit, Eva, where are you?"

"Right here."

His heart couldn't take much more. It dropped to his stomach, and before either of them could say anything, he crushed her to his chest.

"I was so worried. Brad told me he upset you. Are you okay?" He pulled back to look at her.

"I'm fine. I just needed a time out. I overreacted. It was stupid."

His hands slid down her arms. "I'm so glad you came back."

She pulled free from his embrace and turned away. "How did it go with your ex? You two gonna renew your vows?"

"Eva," he put his hand on her shoulder, "I can't get back together with her because I'm falling for you."

She looked over her shoulder at him, a smile teasing the corners of her lips. "Are you now?"

"I know it's quick, and you'll need more time, but I'm willing to take it slow."

"Christmas Eve Give." She wrapped her arms around his waist.

He wrinkled his forehead. It took him a

second to process. "Anything you want, name it. I'll get it for you."

"Even if I ask for the moon?" she asked, eyebrows raised.

"Especially if you ask for that." He slid her hands down to the curve of his rump.

"When I told you I'd love you forever, I was only kidding a little. I could, you know?"

"I'm pretty sure I want you to." He kissed her sweet lips and moved her toward the bed.

"Wait."

"You need a time out?"

"No, I need to let my family know where I am."

Adam dialed Brad. "She's with me. We'll be over in time for dinner." He tossed the phone before he kicked the bedroom door shut.

No woman had ever looked at him with caring in her eyes like Eva did. It was the kind of love that could carry a man across miles of uneven ground.

CHAPTER TWELVE

Eva cleared away the dessert dishes while Adam helped the kids pick out cookies to leave for Santa. When the children were in bed, the adults settled around the fireplace to plan Santa's delivery. Adam handed her a mug of hot apple cider before sitting next to her, his spine rigid.

Brad and Uncle Charlie seemed to be disagreeing about something, talking with closed lips. It was strange because Adam had also argued with Brad before dinner, but she didn't know what about.

"What's up?" Eva asked, looking back and forth between them.

"They're trying to decide which news to give you." Her aunt's face was full of sympathy.

"What news?"

"Your mother is dead," Brad blurted and snatched an envelope away from his dad.

Eva looked down for a second, trying to

decide how she would allow the news to affect her. A thousand images flashed in her head of the woman who'd given birth to her, none of them good.

"No, she's not." She looked at Aunt Lynn. "My real mother is sitting right here, alive and well. I've never called you that because I wasn't sure you wanted me to, but you're the woman who taught me what a wife and mom are supposed to be. I can't thank you enough for everything you've done for me."

"Oh, my sweet girl." Aunt Lynn cried and hugged her.

When things were calm, Eva took a steadying breath. "What's the other news?"

Adam closed his eyes and rubbed her back. Whatever it was, he didn't look thrilled about it.

Brad handed her an envelope with her name on it, written in Mickey's precise block lettering.

Her heart thumped in her ears. "W-What's this?"

"I should've given it to you sooner, but Mickey gave me specific instructions. He wrote it before his first deployment and asked me to give it to you if he didn't make it back and you had trouble moving on. You're starting to make progress, but I thought you'd want to read it anyway."

"We don't want to upset you on Christmas."

Uncle Charlie's eyes were narrowed with concern. "I wanted Brad to wait to give it to you after."

In a day filled with emotional choices, they kept coming. Would the letter send her back inside herself? Or would it confirm the course she was on?

She glanced at Adam. His jaw worked side to side.

"You don't want me to read this?" she asked.

His eyes widened as his mouth opened. "I…" He took a breath. "I want you to be happy. If reading it upsets you, I don't want that."

She held the letter out to him. "You read it and tell me if there's anything I can't live without knowing."

He squinted his eyes. "Are you sure?"

"If it can wait until after Christmas, you let me know." She pushed it into his hand, still torn.

Adam used the letter opener Aunt Lynn gave him. He unfolded the paper and read.

Eva wiped her sweaty palms on her pants and listened to Bing Crosby sing "White Christmas" on the radio. She'd always love Mickey, but he wasn't here anymore, and she had a lot of living to do. She didn't want to do it alone.

Adam put his arm around her and kissed her

temple. "You're not going to believe this." He handed her the paper.

She looked at him for a long moment, and with his reassuring nod, she held her breath and fixed her eyes on the page.

Eva,

If you're reading this, I didn't make it and you're grieving too much. Know that more than anything, I wanted to come home to you, but sometimes God has other plans.

By now, you've cussed me a hundred times for leaving you and you've sworn to yourself there'll never be another man for you, but you're wrong. You're too young and beautiful to stay single—that's why I scooped you up when I had the chance. You've got the biggest heart in the world and too much love to give to keep it locked away. Open it and let the right one in. You'll know him because he'll want to give you the moon, but he'll know you'd be just as happy having your hand held beneath it.

It's time to dry your eyes and return to active duty. I'm not there, but you don't need me to be. Get on with it.

I love you more,

Your Mickey "Mouse"

Eva wiped her face, where tears had left their tracks, before she turned to Adam and smiled, her heart full.

He pulled her into his arms and kissed the

top of her head. "I'm your guy, he said so."

***

Adam watched Eva sleep as the sun was beginning to rise on Christmas morning. His days of hating the dawn seemed to be behind him.

When she opened her eyes, he said, "Christmas Give."

Her smile spread and she stroked his face with her fingertips. "What's your wish?"

He reached across her and grabbed his letter to Santa. "Read this."

She read it aloud. "Dear Santa, I want this Christmas to last forever." She looked at him. "Me too, but I'm not sure how to make that happen. I could wear my little hat every day."

"You carry holiday cheer with you." He touched the spot over her heart. "Say you'll be with me, that you've got my back."

"It's a mighty big back, and I'm such a tiny little thing." She laughed before her face got serious. "Adam, I'm honored you want me on your team. I won't let you down."

Words failed him, so he kissed her. It would've led to more, except Brad knocked on the door. The kids were waiting on them to arrive, so they could open presents.

The four of them, Bella included, rode together. They sipped coffee while the kids tore through their Santa gifts. Adam grinned at

Savannah's reaction to her new Barbie. Eva nudged him and winked. In that moment, he saw into their future—Christmas mornings with excited kids, hairy dogs, and aggravating uncles. Eva would be the perfect mother for his children.

She pulled gifts from her stocking, which hung from the mantle next to his. There were three bottles of red nail polish and lots of chocolate. Bella's stocking had more treats than she could eat in a month. Adam's had oranges, pecans, and a red mankini with white fur around the waistline.

"That's to match your hat." Brad pointed to his head as his lips twisted to fight a grin.

Adam gave Eva her first gift from him. She danced around holding the espresso maker close to her chest. On the second present, she peeled back the paper and stared into the box.

She put her hand on her chest and looked up at him. "The Bahamas?"

"Brad told me you didn't have to go back to work until after the New Year, so next week, you and me, sun and slides."

"It sounds wonderful, but…"

His heart thumped in his chest. She'd made other plans. She'd changed her mind.

"Well, I was going to round up some big strong men to help me load a moving truck."

Lynn yelled. "You're moving back."

"Yeah, I'm kinda unemployed at the moment."

Adam wondered if it was okay to be so happy about her news. She'd want to find a job soon, but he wished she'd just let him take care of her for a little while.

"Where are you going to live, Aunt Eva?" Savannah straddled her legs.

"She's going to stay with me until we find her a place." Brad looked pointedly at Adam.

Adam nodded at his friend who'd also invited him to stay indefinitely until he found his own house. With any luck, he and Eva might be picking out a home together.

He stroked her hair. "We'll get you moved when we get back from the trip, all right?"

Brad cleared his throat. "Cuz, don't you have a rich boyfriend who could hire movers for you?"

She looked at Adam. "I don't know or care what his bank account looks like, all I know is he's rich where it counts." She tapped the center of his chest.

Adam kissed her. She was better than any cheerleader who ever routed for a team. She was his Christmas Give.

EPILOGUE

Christmas morning the following year...

The family was seated around the den, surrounded by mounds of torn wrapping paper and bows.

Savannah perched on Adam's lap, holding a baby doll in one arm. "I asked Santa for y'all to get married, but I guess he didn't have time for that this year."

Eva tried to suppress her smile. "Actually, we've got news."

Uncle Charlie bowed up. "Am I gonna have to get the shotgun?"

"No, sir." Adam beamed. "Although, we are expecting..."

Gasps, yips, and murmurs filled the pine scented air. Savannah got up and danced around. Eva retrieved the ring from her pocket, and Adam took it from her and slid it on her finger.

"I talked her into it when we were in the Bahamas in September." He kissed the band on her finger.

Brad shot to his feet. "You waited three months to tell us?"

"We were going to tell y'all at Thanksgiving, but I found out I was pregnant right before." She smiled at her new husband and squeezed his leg. "We wanted a little time to enjoy it, just us."

Brad sat back down and put his arm around Andrea. "Well, if it's a boy, you better name him after me, since I'm the reason y'all are together."

"You gonna have a whole litter of football players, Aunt Eva?" Zack tossed his football in the air and caught it.

Eva put her hands on her belly and looked down. "I want my boys to play a real manly sport, like hockey. None of this sissy football business."

Adam tackled her gently by wrapping his arms and a leg around her and rolling them from their seat onto the floor. He kissed her all over her face and neck, while she squirmed and laughed. Bella joined in the fun and bit Adam's pant leg.

"T-Time," Eva called, breathless.

"Now we can call you Mack-Daddy." Brad did his victory dance.

While the family bounced around and celebrated, Eva cupped Adam's cheek. "Best Christmas Give ever."

ABOUT THE AUTHOR

Meda White is an award-winning author who writes sweet, funny, southern romance. Born with Georgia clay running through her veins, she continues to enjoy the heat and humidity of the South with her

Hubba-luv and furbabies—Lily, a very sweet yet spoiled Collie, and Lulu, the cat with one fang. When not writing, you might find her making music, shooting zombie targets, teaching fitness, or explaining the meaning of her unusual first name.

DEDICATION

In loving memory of the world's greatest grandmothers.
I can still hear "*Christmas Give*" in my mind.
Grandma—a.k.a. Verna Taylor Phillips
Maw—a.k.a. Eva Odom Faircloth

ACKNOWLEDGMENTS

To my editor, Andrea Grimm, thank you for believing in me and helping me make my stories the best they can be. Many thanks.

A NOTE TO READERS

Dear Reader,

Thank you for reading *Christmas Give*. I hope you enjoyed Eva & Adam's love story.

If you have a moment to leave an honest review, I'd really appreciate it. Not only do reviews let authors know how they're doing, they help readers find new books.

Please look for me on my Website and my Dirt Road Darlings Facebook reader group.

Thank you and best wishes for a lifetime of love and laughter.

Meda

OTHER TITLES FROM MEDA WHITE

The Southland Romance Series

Home With My Heart (The Prequel)

Play With My Heart (Book 1)

Dance With My Heart (Book 2)

Ride With My Heart (Book 3)

Fool With My Heart (Book 4)

The Southern College Novellas

Spring Fling

Fall Rush

Winter Formal